Hunger to Share

Hunger to Share

Poems

Peg Bresnahan

Press 53
Winston-Salem

Press 53, LLC
PO Box 30314
Winston-Salem, NC 27130

First Edition

Copyright © 2019 by Peg Bresnahan

All rights reserved, including the right of reproduction in whole or in part in any form except in the case of brief quotations embodied in critical articles or reviews. For permission, contact publisher at editor@Press53.com, or at the address above.

Cover Art, "Flowers and Candle Floating" © Neosiam 2017. Licensed through iStock.

Cover design by Christopher Forrest and Kevin Morgan Watson

Library of Congress Control Number
2019934223

Printed on acid-free paper
ISBN 978-1-950413-02-7

To my community of friends who share the wonder of poetry and, as always, for Dan, my companion on life's surprising journey.

The author gratefully acknowledges the following journals in which these poems, occasionally in different versions, first appeared:

Ekphrasis, "Firebird"

The Great Smokies Review, "One the Outskirts of Phnom Penh," "Irvie," "To the woman who said, Deer are like rats, they are everywhere."

Kakalak, "A Hard Left," "The Tower of Silence," "Esterio's Dinner Party," "In the Hills of Sri Lanka"

NC Literary Review, "Knife Lake," "Auricles"

Poetry in Plain Sight, "The Swimmer"

Raleigh Review, "Wisteria"

What Matters, "Girl in a Red Dress"

"Auricles" was named a finalist for the James Applewhite Poetry Prize and nominated for Best of the Net.

Contents

Picking Threads off a Lover

Auricles	3
When I fell in love the second time	4
Picking Threads off a Lover	5
Rust	6
Lake Clara	7
after champagne	8
To the woman who said, *Deer are like rats,*	
they are everywhere.	10
Picking Up Litter along Sky Valley Road	11
Commodity	12
Where Is Chagall?	13
Revelation Revisited	14

Wonders Hidden and Huge

Knife Lake	17
Summer Music	18
Portent	19
Isle Royale	20
Chicken Bone Lake	21
Skin	22
Night Walk	23
A Small Piece of the World	24

Fringe of Magic Carpet

From the Budget Rental Renault	27
Esterio's Dinner Party	28
Christmas Concert at the Ladies College	
in Colombo	29
Girl in a Red Dress	30
In the Hills of Sri Lanka	31
Wisteria	32
Rickshaw through the Night	33
On the Outskirts of Phnom Penh	34
Tower of Silence	35
Mumbai	36
A Hard Left	37

THE OTHER SIDE OF AIR

Firebird   41
A Tree Holds Its Stories Close   42
Swimming with My Mother's Melanoma   43
The Mortician Explains   44
Finding Jeff   45
Irvie   46
Man in a Stetson Cowboy Hat   47
Regrets Only   48
The Greatest Generation Passes It On   49

ENORMOUS THINGS

World of One Thousand Greens   53
On Deck   54
The Orange and Green Pig Barge   55
Tips to Remove and Replace Wrecked Propellers   56
View from the Pig Barge   57
The Beijing Puppeteer   58
Slow Barge to China   59
Laotian Customs Officer   60
In Dreams It's Sailing Backward   61
Our Last Night   62

Notes   65

About the Author   67

Picking Threads off a Lover

The longest journey is the journey inward.
—Dag Hammarskjöld

Auricles

When the cat hid one of your hearing aids
in my hiking boot, I walked down the trail
with its rub. My big toe heard a mole
tunnel among sassafras roots, a rabbit

thump its warning. We don't have conversations
the way we once did. No longer
do I ask a question from another room,
talk with my back turned. Now, it's face

to face. When the phone rings for you,
I walk rooms, hallways, rap on closed doors.
Absurd to be annoyed when I cannot
imagine you gone, the house an echo,

your office a space for guests. Do you know
at night, when I round the corner
into our room, the first thing I look for
is the hill of your feet beneath the sheet?

When I fell in love the second time

I fastened onto a pop song
                to describe my feelings.

                It was bizarre
since now I can't recall the title   or who sang it

but nothing described how I felt
                except those words   that melody.

Music does that

in movies   commercials
                about returning soldiers, coffee, mothers with moist eyes.

My throat closes and of course it has nothing
to do with TV
                but a moment I'd swoon to repeat, or

one of my selfish decisions I thought I'd erased
         only to feel the prick of the pitchfork.

Dan told me when he was in Memphis
              he toured Graceland on a lark.

Women seventy and eighty were sobbing over Elvis

              in the meditation and rose gardens
under magnolia trees
         all over the grounds.

A guard said it was that way every day.

Picking Threads off a Lover

But you know, I'd rather write
how refugees risk death on seas, their fingers
clenched around anything that floats.
I'd rather write about the environment,
or a safe from the Titanic—photos,
jewelry, letters—12,000 feet below
the two of us, you on the porch
expounding, one hand holding up
a bath towel tucked around your waist,
the other gesticulating to emphasize
whatever started our quarrel,
my theatrical exit directing me to the Subaru,
strike toward I haven't a clue where,
my love for you leaping out open windows,
loose on the macadam, hungry for air.

Rust

After dinner and wine,
I said you looked bored
listening to me talk
about the book on thirty-three
Chilean miners trapped
two thousand feet underground
for sixty-seven days.

You said if a shrink were here
he'd ask you, *are you always
bored with what she's saying?*

This morning you told me
I walked out of the kitchen
while you were still talking
about your book on rust.

I didn't remember,
which proved we were both guilty.
I started to laugh but you retorted
corrosion, as a major
problem, fascinated you.

I thought of Minneapolis,
its buckled bridge—or me
driving off the bridge
in Duluth on my way to work,
the Subaru and me
upside down in Lake Superior.

Perhaps that's why
I've always crossed bridges
with car windows open
even if it's thirty below, why I keep
a sledgehammer in my car
just in case.

Lake Clara

Dan leans into a rhythm.
The oars dip and lift. The shore
slides by—a moving diorama—
one pier, birches, willows.
Water so clear
I see sand twenty feet down.
In a bog around the bend,
coontail and duckweed thicken.

Sandhill cranes
forage for frogs and crayfish.
Five feet, slate gray,
the male with crimson crown.

These days, everyone I love,
my every belief, feels threatened.
To see a species whose fossils
lie beside woolly mammoths'
and saber-toothed tigers'
is a forty-million-year-old promise.
The birds' footsteps send watery rings.

after champagne

it's their anniversary
and he asks her
if she's happy
a word crammed

with all the years
they've loved each other
over four children's heads
yes   plans were hijacked

*

kill those seconds
on the dark beach road
then   their daughter's car will not
hit the man in jeans
and black jacket
she will not
leave death behind her

whisk her from a cage
the metal clank of echoes
far from jumpsuits

dress her in t-shirt
shorts   tevas   on the trail
to buckhorn creek
climbing the ridge
through hemlocks
on rays of sun

*

bicycle home on the sidewalk
then   the trucker won't leave him
sprawled beneath the traffic lights
at the intersection
blood stuck to his skin

leave before midnight
the trauma nurse won't tell her
he had beautiful red hair
except it was brown

part of his chef's brain eclipsed
his taste and smell for salt
spices   gone

their café closes
and they climb   night
balanced on one shoulder
day on the other
his brain collating clues

she passes that intersection
at least four times a day
four times a day
imagines driving over
his chalked outline

    *

the moment he asks
if she is happy
tumbles
through the hourglass

she replies
i will hold you
    you hold me

To the woman who said, *Deer are like rats,*
they are everywhere.

Her eyes flared terror.
Her hooves scrabbled the mountain road,
fastened to the double yellow line
as if it led home.

The thud against the fender felt huge.
My flashers warned the world to stop.
I bolted out, dropped to my knees,
stroked spots no older than two months.

I prayed for a god, any god
to place her in the bowl of sky so at night
everyone would see her
bounding beside Pegasus.

Watched her wildness slide.

Picking Up Litter along Sky Valley Road

Bud Light, a few Red Bull cans,
        hubcap, carpet attachment for a Hoover.

Beside a fenced-in field with two donkeys
        and a tribe of fainting goats,
                a Mason jar labeled *Watermelon Moonshine*.

You may think home-brewed, corn ground to mush,
        coils of copper soldered to a still near a stream.
                But I see lunar light, the black-seeded smile

of a red-haired witch
        sweeping the sky with her broom,
                the glow of a strawberry moon.

Where Is Chagall?

    Dan grabs my ankle
we float up
    side down

    riding a rooster

because it's Saturday
    wings paint the feeder

        lady-slippers
kick off their shoes

our wildflower fingers

    strew fistfuls of forget-me-nots

  over fields   farms a funeral
    procession with its car lights on

twelve miles
seat-belted bumper-
to-bumper to Walmart
for five smoke
detectors, a toilet handle

    we need a goat

      a mauve violin

Commodity

Crankie's is now The Horseshoe Café.
The floors are still concrete.
Paula lined the walls with local artists'
paintings, some matted with fabric
to soak up sound. If you call ahead,
Sherwood Forest's nine-hole golf course
rents lamas as caddies. Dixie Produce,
open only in warm months, resold
to a couple from Colorado
who know nothing about okra,
greens or peaches. Cars and trucks
bristle kayaks and bicycles, clog Crab Creek Road.
We were so proud of the forest—its history,
waterfalls, moss-coated boulders,
the creatures calling it home.
We spread the word—forgot
how connected we are to the earth
until we pull it apart.
Maps, brochures, website, fund-raising tours,
our zeal lit wires. Of course
people came—some only to study the angles.
We saw it as teacher, a wilderness
to protect, pass on with respect—never
considered it a commodity to conquer.
Now miracles flatten under
the weight of agendas. For every trail
and gravel road, more trees fall.

Revelation Revisited

Michelangelo painted the saved and the damned
in the skin they left behind.

They're here—the dead resurrected,
dressed—in our house, our yard, our garage.

No golden bowls of incense, collapsed stars.
The storm cellar doors fly open.

Dante strides toward the house,
souls from the circles cling to his cloak.

On the porch, Galileo peers through his telescope,
trashing old theories, discovering new.

Stallions pour from Ruben's brush, hooves and manes
of cumulus flare so close I smell burnt silver.

Bach composes a suite for cello,
Vivaldi, his chin on a violin.

Concertos for harpsichord
slide over my freshly waxed floor.

St. Jude, patron saint of desperate causes, sweeps into the room.
He knows what lies behind

that pulsing skin of sky ready to rupture.
In our kitchen the walls turn red.

Wonders Hidden and Huge

*Frogs discovered their national anthem again.
I didn't know a ditch could hold so much joy.*
—William Stafford

Knife Lake

Come out here. Look at the constellations,
how the sky weeps stories that mimic our own.

Or the crescent moon cradling a shadowed pearl
called earthshine. I'm not sure I know

what I'm talking about, but I love the idea
I can see moon's back. Who knows what she's hiding?

Last week I spotted a pouch suspended from a low
laurel branch, half an inch of water in its egg-sized tear.

I marked it with a tepee of sticks, clicked a photo,
sent it to everyone I knew.

Sunday, I led our congregation to a luna moth and a cluster
of imperials. Wind wrinkled the luna's sleeves

as it clung to a pine window frame. Yellow and brown
imperials painted a path like autumn leaves.

Who needs an angel when miracles surround us?
Up in the Boundary Waters, I woke my tent mate.

We sat at the edge of Knife Lake zipped in sleeping bags,
sipped wine, oohed and aahed until Aurora Borealis unplugged.

If I'm the last creature alive, no matter what shape
earth is in, and I discover a wonder hidden or huge,

I know I'll panic, break into an icy sweat with the hunger to share.
My tongue will swell with the intensity of untelling.

Summer Music

Right outside our back door,
the little brown, upside down,
sated, asleep in carport rafters
after a meal of beetles and mosquitoes.

At an evening lawn concert last month,
scalloped shadows swooped Mahler's First.
Moths, mayflies, lacewings, vanished in an arabesque
among riggings of light and sound,
a conductor wielding his baton.

Portent

I dreamed a unicorn
the size of a warbler.
It knelt inside a bird's nest
drinking from eggshells
the color of camouflage.

The moon hooks its horn
over the mountain,
borrows the sun
to light its own lantern.

When will we learn
not to applaud
the taste of plunder,
the sound of hooves
as they paw, maraud?

Isle Royale

I smell the odor
nylon takes on when folded damp.
Inside our sleeping bag
I press close, watch your eyelids flick,
wonder what dreams they cover.

        Chippewa,
              Sioux,
thimbleberries, moose, eagle plumes.

I think of the women, babies swaddled, lashed in cradle
boards to their backs.

I'd fall short.
              But for a week,
house and bed strapped to my shoulders,
I follow you across birch bogs,
swamplands, the Greenstone Ridge,
a canoe upended on your back.

Chicken Bone Lake

I crouched at lake's edge, sloshed water
    over my face, so frigid, full
        of iron I smelled a foundry

forged in umber through trunks, branches
    drowned in muck. So what if it's been
        thirty years? The memory

returns when cold water hits my eyes,
    Why not begin mornings
        with the mesmerizing tremolo

of loons, dawn's frescoed sky—
    birch and spruce netted with mist?
        I towel my face—porcelain

sink, granite countertop, clay
    soap dish shaped like a leaf, heated
        tiles beneath my feet

Skin

Volts of dry lightning split the seams of night,
fork the mountains around us. This morning
Dan found a fresh copperhead skin
against the rocks, yards from our front door.

I thought of our own old cells, millions
sloughed each minute.
Every six weeks a fresh coat,
an added wrinkle or bruise. If we were like snakes,

skins shed whole as we grew, our closets
would be stuffed with younger, smaller selves.
I've read they're transplanting chimps' brains.

If true, somewhere in a clinic
in the Alps, a billionaire bids adieu to plastic knees,
hearing aids, his brain slipped into a man,
stitches hidden beneath
a mop of dark hair.

Just when his old form was comfortable, edges
soft as favorite sweats, he zips into a twenty
year old, his cerebrum filled with hindsight,
bursting to do it right—this time with style.

Night Walk

My flashlight caught the snake
on the driveway
stretched out,
seeping up the day's leftover heat.
Difficult to identify
by a circle of light.

In nightgown and flip flops
I wasn't going closer
to check for slit pupils,
arrowhead face, telltale pits.

It side-winded toward rocks
vertebrae and muscle
into the joe-pye weed
cloaked in the last sun
like a new skin.

A Small Piece of the World

These mountains once rose taller than Everest.
Ada, ninety-five, said when her daddy was a boy,
a mail route ran through here.
Not far from where moonshine was brewed.
Both gone now, smothered by laurel,
galax, rhododendron. She seemed
to remember she was Baptist—went mute.

Buckhorn Creek, at times pure
energy soaking low hanging branches, slides,
mirrors hemlocks, sweet gums, chinquapins.

I'll hike back after dark
and read sky charts, search for Cygnus.
The swan's brightest stars mark the Northern Cross.
With luck I'll see them
in that clear pool above the falls.

Fringe of Magic Carpet

*There is no end to the adventures that we can have
if only we seek them with our eyes open.*
—Jawaharlal Nehru

From the Budget Rental Renault

It is a mural and I am in it.
Crumbled aqueducts punctuate pastures.

Temple remnants frame
wheat fields, fallen columns.

The occasional camel
and I am Biblical.

Women on their way to harvest vegetables
stand like float queens in open trucks.

A few swathed in black
shadow their sisters.

Everywhere I see children.
Small herders chase goats

and cows with sticks.
Some stand along the roadside

and wave. One so young
she drags a scrap of blanket.

Barefoot in the dust
clouded sun, we watch each other.

Horses haul wagons.
As we pass

hay tilts and teeters.
Golden explosions.

Esterio's Dinner Party

Castro naked, save his army cap,
sketched and fired onto stark white porcelain,
women, knees and legs so far apart
their toes could hook each end of Cuba.

One thousand dollars buys a plate
in a courtyard of lemon trees and fig.
Two hundred copulating Fidels
in forty-eight poses aped the Kama Sutra
on tables, mounted
to walls around the buffet.

      I look, try
not to look,
to look
blasé.
      Esterio's Delphic drawings,
a dictator screwing his country
      every which way.

Where to place the shredded flank
steak in tomato sauce? The yellow rice,
fried potato balls, the yucca?

Christmas Concert at the Ladies College in Colombo

Because we're near the equator
and it's Christmas among Buddhists,
there are no tinseled trees, poinsettias.
Instead we're in an auditorium.

Men in tan suits, women sheathed in saris—
ruby, emerald, gold. Barbara and I
in sensible suitcase clothes,
two sparrows in an aviary of exotic plumes.

Fifty young women face us on risers,
one thick black braid falling to each waist.

Carols in the sultry air swirl the room.
O come let us adore Him—the sounds
close my throat. *Hark! the herald angels sing*—

I'm driving down Michigan Avenue toward midnight
mass, a manger scene and candles, past homes
glittering with lights in snow-covered bushes.

How not to stand for Handel opening his soul?
Barbara and I rise. The couple in front of us
does too. It's a ripple effect
like the wave at soccer games back home.

Girl in a Red Dress

Far out at sea the wave sucked itself back as if gathering strength,
held there, while the people ran out to marvel at a sand floor
they'd never seen. Some gathered fish and conch;
others dragged out chairs staking claim to more land.

It has been years since the seabed slipped and fell to its knees
unleashing a crescendo of energy that roared like a jet toward the beach
and reared, a wall of water taller than the tallest palm, close as my car
parked outside the museum. Two rooms, one light bulb, a gallon jar

for donations, partitions plastered with torn, mud-faded photographs.
Families and friends, arms thrown across each other's shoulders,
around waists, cheek-to-cheek, hand-in-hand, fixed by a click
onto paper squares. *The wave came for them,* my guide says.

I follow her outside to a hut flanked by flattened grass and two cows.
Inside is hot. Dark. She flicks on a flashlight. Drawings are pasted
and tacked to the walls, small survivors coloring their memories.

On one sheet, a girl in a red dress clutches a spotted dog,
her black braids flying. The background is slate-colored, its caption,
my friend Maulie. Drawings of clothing, boats, people, all tangled in trees,
upside down train cars, arms and legs dangling from their windows.

Stick figures tumble through a maelstrom of indigo, ocher, umber,
their mouths a slash or a circle. I pause to look out the door,

across the road to stalls selling snapper and king coconuts. Behind them,
fishing boats in primary colors rock on a surface that barely ripples.

In the Hills of Sri Lanka

What I didn't count on—no electricity,
no hot water, no eating after noon.

I didn't know there was no
reading, writing, talking.

Leeches in wet grass.
Rats in rafters above toilets and showers.

Not sure why I left Kandy—goodbye to saris,
sarongs, bare feet and flip-flops, carts, cars, bicycles,
goats, elephants, monkeys, all of us sheened
with oily hues of diesel, dust and sweat

to follow the long song of a gong, balance my head
on its ladder of spine, winnow stones from rice,
sweep dirt paths above a panorama of pepper plants.

Not easy to empty my mind when I'm the only
one who knows the world's in a state
of collapse.

Ignore the fire in rat's eyes,
do not trip on the tail.
It drags like a scythe.

Wisteria

Purple flowers
swaying in the dark,
fall from the slender waists
of seven celestial sisters.
Their fragrance finds a wife
in Pakistan, caged
by windows filigreed
in iron. Swathed
in veils of dust and gas,
she dreams galactic cuffs
around her wrists,
her hair on fire.

Rickshaw Through the Night

    Varanasi

Bicycles pull rickshaws. It is 10 o'clock.
My driver pedals over broken roads
lit by bonfires and dim bulbs, around people
bundled asleep under clusters of umbrellas,
beneath banyan trees.

We pass cattle, closed shops, goats, dogs.
The air feels soiled, scratched with dust.
Dan is in a rickshaw ahead of me.
I grab the sides of mine.

The last mile we walk surrounded
by thousands here to honor the Ganges.
I breathe body heat, diesel, dung,
sandalwood smoke. My ears fill
with the din of strange words.

I grab Dan's hand. We climb down stepped
landings into a wooden skiff looped
with swags of marigolds and are rowed away
from India's holiest city.

I look back at color unleashed—more bonfires,
painted turrets, steeples topped with weather
vanes, flags, banners. Small lights
garland balconies, canopies.
Painted ads scrawl buildings
in a language of swoops and swirls.

Beside the river people sit on the landings
and talk. Others around plastic tables
or in groups on reed mats. A nasal-toned
singer plucks his sitar.

Worshipers recite Sanskrit verses,
splash handfuls of the Ganges over their faces.
We glide away from the brilliance.
Night flattens, mutes to gray.
A smell of smoke yokes the air to the river.

On the Outskirts of Phnom Penh

Six thousand paper faces stuck to the walls
of what was a school—a record in black and white
of those about to be tortured by boys
trained in interrogation.

Classrooms are as they were found—
each with one desk and chair, a steel bed frame,
shackles at both ends.
A metal bar to hold the victim down.

*

Thousands were stuffed into trucks,
bludgeoned in an orchard to save bullets.
Mass graves, special pits for children.

Even now, nooses hang from trees. A glass tower
is full of skulls. After the rains,
the soil weeps bone, teeth, pieces of fabric.

*

They came for me, took me to a boy's compound.
I was twelve—in charge of a cow. If I brought her
back at dusk, I lived. One day the cow disappeared.

I crawled through a rice field. It belched rancid odors.
A forest of chankiri trees. That's where I found her.

Loudspeakers rigged to the trees blared sounds of heavy
machinery mixed with music to smother the screams.

I still hear it.

Tower of Silence

The vultures wait.
They are always waiting, a dark
gyre of hunger.

The Parsee believe earth and water are pure,
fire is divine, ancient elements must not
be polluted with decay.

For three thousand years, from Persia to India,
the birds have devoured bodies sleeved
in nothing but skin, food for a six-foot wingspan
that widens and soars.

Acres of orchids, frangipani, bodhi,
banyan and mahogany surround a tower
tall enough to be seen for miles.

From the hotel balcony, I watch
the silent shapes—dive, rise, dive
to the tower's roof.
I'm told it takes less than an hour.

Mumbai

Six-foot wings ride the air.
Their shadows skim the Mahalaxmi Bridge
where we peer down into a diorama
of slum labor.

The dark shapes spread over men
pushing wooden trolleys heaped with bulging
bags, over hand scrubbers knee-deep
in soapy water. Thrashers wallop water
out of towels against a flogging stone.

The sun hisses.
Sweat pastes our pants and shirts flat.

The "world's largest outdoor laundry"
is as foreign to us as the Tower of Silence
where the Parsee have honored earth,
air, fire and water for three thousand years.

To honor the elements, they place their naked
dead on top of the tower for vultures,
what these birds were born to do.

Bundles of clean laundry are picked up
for delivery, soiled bags dropped off.
Eight thousand workers live, work, die here,
will wash and dry for the rest of their lives.

A Hard Left

Raise a glass to Francie.
She grabbed a fringe of magic carpet and flew
straight out of Raleigh to Istanbul,
marrying a man she'd met six weeks before.

He was young enough to be her grandson.
Probably wanted a Green Card.
After her money.

She didn't care.
Didn't care that before he sold rugs
he'd been a shepherd from a village
with three diacritical marks in its name.

She gave up wine and weed, shed weight.
What would you do? What would I,
if a stranger asked us to wrench a hard left
away from days so familiar
we didn't have to open our eyes?

Don't we all carry a talisman—vial of sand,
scrap of peau de soie, strip of horizon?
Turn around and we might see our old
familiar past loaded with a sack of tired
desire trudging behind, then picture Francie

in clickety wooden sandals and a fringed
cotton pestemal, headed into a steamy tiled
hamam, or ferrying across the Bosporus
between continents to purchase pistachios
at the Spice Bazaar.

Cheer her on as she nails an indigo glass
evil eye to their front door to deflect calamity,
learns to stuff grape leaves, drink yogurt water,
calls what was once a sloe-eyed
illusion, *my husband*.

THE OTHER SIDE OF AIR

*With soaring head I'll strike the stars
of heaven.*
—Horace

Firebird

He sketched onto the sheet of steel
with a stick of soapstone, erased,
repeated for days, weeks,
but she spun out of reach.
If the forms didn't match
what he saw behind his eyes,
cutting torch in hand he tried again.

He welded. She began to sway.
Pirouettes, passés, pliés,
he couldn't keep up.
Wreathed in flame,
she raised her arms,
ecstatic in the welder's light.
Golden feathers lit the shop.

A Tree Holds Its Stories Close

The Swimmer waited inside a Spanish oak,
a rectangular slab, three feet by two.
He chiseled, carved, sanded,
in constant conversation with the wood.
For the sculptor, grain, edges,
knots dictated form.

It took weeks before he recognized her
from a photo seventy years ago.
Hollow shape smooth as liquid
where a heart once kept pace,
through the mist, strokes cleaved water,
clear as a loon's call.

Swimming with My Mother's Melanoma

Till the End of Time pours through the speakers
around Mom's pool.

She loves to tell the story, how on his way home
from the war in '45, Dad called from a pay phone

at a bar in Philadelphia, sang this song
straight through. By the time he finished

he was out of quarters, line dead.
She's exercising in the shallow end, a morning routine

at ninety-three she won't quit.
Her hands swish the surface. She smiles at me

while we croon along with Perry Como, but I'll bet
she sees herself in the backyard with friends long gone,

all barefoot on the lawn, swinging to James,
Basie, Goodman, high heels and wingtips

wedged between branches of the flowering crab apple,
forever after called the shoe tree.

Pearl Harbor, Normandy—nightmares smothered
with music, laughter, brandy Manhattans.

The Mortician Explains

*Her coffin will slide
into a chamber, flames
rising from fourteen
to eighteen hundred degrees.
After two and a half hours
I scoop her skeleton
into a special blender
and pulverize,
sift the metal and plastic
from her hip and back.*

I think about Mom's favorite
turquoise silk blouse
and skirt she wore,
the stockings and girdle
she refused to be without
that held her together.

Finding Jeff

After the blizzard, a polar vortex cut through town.
Thermometers plunged to forty below,

coldest New Year's Eve anyone under fifty could remember.
A news photographer spotted the ghost of a car left

too close to the lake, carved by waves into sculpture.
I saw it on TV and remembered Jeff,

a boy I hadn't thought about in thirty years.
Not my son, thank God, the only child of Mary Ann and Lee.

Seventeen. There'd been a party.
He never came home.

His parents made phone calls, questioned friends.
For hours, volunteers in snowmobile suits,

armed with flashlights, slid over frozen walks,
floundered through drifts around trees sleeved in ice.

A stone sun cracked the sky.
Below the bluff, Lake Michigan waited,

a world of white stretched above her skin.
Who knew why Jeff was down there.

A fist of wind spinning him over the edge
through brittle brush that snapped and tore?

Chain saws, pickaxes—it took hours to free him.
A sweep of spray, his mouth crystal.

Irvie

When Irvie returned home to Chicago after D-Day,
he drove a delivery truck from the Union Stockyard
slaughterhouse to butcher shops around the city.

He steered that old truck, hauled the same smells
of fear he'd breathed for forty years, kept abattoirs
locked inside his temporal lobe, the memories

a tag around his neck—mines, German steel
tetrahedrons wedged in sand along shore, ramps,
barbed wire, shrapnel still black in his back.

Man in a Stetson Cowboy Hat

My aunt and two cousins flew with his pipe-dream
wherever it tugged—Brazil, Panama, Cuba—
three tails tied to his kite.

Photos arrived by mail.
Uncle John, bareback on a palomino, shirt
opened four buttons, high-laced boots, or

slashing sugarcane with his machete.
In one black and white, he holds a folded dead
fer-de-lance to his mouth in a snake-skin grin.

Always—women
looking his way. Last night, I dreamed when he kissed
my aunt, a vireo the size of a baby's thumbnail

stood in his eye.
Its beak unraveled the iris
like a spool of wire.

Regrets Only

Howard, how could you do this to me?
I have to freeze rhubarb and take Rhoda
to the dentist. The Everlasting Mausoleum
on Tuesday is not in my day planner.

When I go, it'll be a class act.
No cut-offs and Clemson t-shirt
in Wal-Mart's pet aisle among the chew toys,
guppies watching me drop.

A restaurant like Le Bernardin on 51st,
me in my red silk that flares at the knees,
those bell earrings with the rhinestone clappers,
four-inch stilettos, sipping Dom Perignon.

Get even for your ignoble exit, Howard.
Haunt confessionals, locker rooms,
wedding suites. There are pluses
in the fourth dimension.

The Greatest Generation Passes It On

Cars race past our last home.
We wave, call from wheelchairs,
wish someone

would look up, see more
than gray hair, loose skin,
stop for coffee, talk.

Then again, there's the worry
if one brakes and turns in,
those behind will follow

like lemmings and our meeting
room will run out of chairs.
Still, the piano bench holds two.

Whoever sits there must
have jukebox fingers,
remember the oldies—Fats,

Miller, Frank, Bing, Dorsey.
The air fueling music
so upbeat with post-war

        promise, three mothers
        driving SUVs might slam on their brakes
        to listen. People locked in seat belts,

        jammed bumper-to-bumper,
        could open windows, thump fists
        on the outside of car doors

        keeping time, except for the teens
        in back of a fire red pick-up—heads
        thrown back, arms, legs wild.

Enormous Things

*Your eyes are small, but
they see enormous things.*
—Rumi

World of One Thousand Greens

Sailing Along the Mekong's Golden Triangle

Flat-bottomed hulls clack, rattle past our riverboat,
all headed for China, carrying a circus of cement,
grain, dried ducks dangling from bamboo poles.

On pig barges men hose animals against the heat.
Spare rudders and propellers roped to pilothouses clank.
An hour later our captain's offering

to the river spirit Naga—incense, banana, saucer
of rice, a glass with wild lilies—rolls off the bow.

To the crew, it's a sign. Animism webs the people
to this world of one thousand greens.

Fairy bush flowers cascade over cliffs, rocks tall
as temples stand along shore or in the water.

Our boat cuts through a river of shallow fury.
We're in our cabin dressing for dinner when the boat jolts.

Lights go out. I stumble, bend to struggle with shoelaces.
Generators rumble. The boat tilts.
Dan grabs pants, shirt, shoes. Throws me a life vest.

On Deck

Dan disappears
in the chaos
among jangles
of language.

I gnaw on the vacuum-
sealed orange vest,
break through, untie
straps—too small.

The pilot's voice
flattens commotion—
*no holes in the hull,
we'll spend tonight*

*slanted, wedged on rock.
The bar is open.*
Find Dan.
Toss a flower to Naga.

The Orange and Green Pig Barge

It pulls alongside.
Boat buddy we decide.
The next morning we climb
over railings, up its steel ladder,
set sail toward a sand spit
in Myanmar.

The sun gasps heat.
We could be in a brochure
for Southeast Asian beaches.

Sixteen passengers from six countries
comb for treasure, play bocce ball.
I skip stones with the Thai chef.

Dan sits on a bright blue plastic
stool close to the water.
One hand holds a shade umbrella,
the other a Singha Gold beer.

He's watching a tug
pull our boat off the rocks,
tow it to the sandbar where we wait.
The crew waits with us,
tools ready.

Tips to Remove and Replace Wrecked Propellers

Grab a hammer. Wade into water that began
as snow trickle off the roof of the world.
Hold your breath, dive.

Feel the river through your veins.
If an ancestor appears, listen to whispers.

Pound, turn, pull the shattered propellers
from their shafts until your liquid breath
thunders for air. Leave the water
for a fire built to heat bones.

Hold the handmade aluminum propellers
and sink through the river's murk again.
Naga's uncoiled around you.

Slide the key into its slot, then the keyway.
Rise and puff out your chest. You fixed two thousand
tons driven by a diesel engine, steel rudders.
Honor the rock.

View from the Pig Barge

A sunset drenches the beach.
It pours over the three novice monks
keeping pace with our barge,
their cotton robes a palette
of cumin, curry, paprika, saffron.

I envy their grins, the energy
in those legs. Their flip-flops
kick up the sand. A fabric of wind
blows it smooth.

Hope pours from the sky.
I want to wring it dry
over my head—possibility, promise
even birdsong filling my pores.

The Beijing Puppeteer

He dangles stars from concealed thread.
A wire moon reflects fire.
There is no sky—only a void
where China's fingers finagle her dams,
yank the Mekong's concrete chains.

Sunrise swells with the serpent's wrath.
The river lord writhes.
Scales rasp against rock.
Villages and farmland
suck chalk along their shores.

Slow Barge to China

From a bench in the stern, I watch Nina
pour water from a bottle into the Mekong,
refill it with wine. The sun blasts full
throttle. Hat low, I slather more SPF 50
on scorched skin. Day five on a pig barge
wasn't on the itinerary.

I'd looked forward to the Menglun Botanical
Gardens with the rare Dragon Tree,
a lute player swathed in peony silk,
while the Dancing Grass swayed.

Instead, we dock below the Laotian customs
kiosk, alongside a flat rock where a family
squats around a freshly butchered pig.
It's possible they live in a village without water,
walked the animal for miles to its slaughter.

We've been told we're the first tourists to arrive
here by water. How strange we must look,
inching over the gunwale, the Mekong to our right,
pigs on our barge to the left. I try not to gag
at the smell, determined not to slip on blood.

Laotian Customs Officer

My kiosk sits on the bluff.
Deities lean from their spirit houses.
I protect the river and the valley
that fans from the water like dragon wings.

Tourists have never left Laos
from the Upper Mekong before.
I was told to expect them in a luxury riverboat.
These people are on a pig barge.

They don't like walking the gunwale.
They step to the rock around the family with a pig
as if they didn't want to touch them.

I cannot allow them to sail to Jing Hong.
The deities agree.

In Dreams It's Sailing Backward

I watch the customs kiosk shrink.
We'll get to China, but not by water.

We saved for this trip, own a home,
car, old truck, dog, two cats.

In this part of the Golden Triangle,
families live in huts smaller
than our carport—no light bulb, faucet.

In my purse—passport, batteries,
eye glass cleaner, antibiotics.

Goodbye to the customs officer,
the family and their butchered pig,
the young monks waving from shore.

Our Last Night

We line up, two by two
on the bow of the ark
assured this will placate Naga.
Wine on our breath,
Dan and I face each other,
grip a bamboo frame
shaped like a lampshade
wrapped in rice paper,
each end open, poised to fly.
The wax fuel cell ignites,
billows light.
Arms stretched high,
we release our fiery plea.
Stranded on a rock
at midnight, in the middle
of the Upper Mekong,
Myanmar on one side,
Laos on the other,
we hold the moon.

Notes

"Esterio's Dinner Party" pg. 28

In 2014, we went to Cuba on an art/architectural tour. In Havana, we were invited to a dinner party at Esterio Segura's living quarters and studio. On display were forty-eight ceramic dinner plates from his show, *48 Glorious Entries of the Victorious Hero into Havana*. Duplicate plates covered the walls. More were set on tables for us to use for dinner. Esterio explained each plate was an avatar of Cuba. What was surprising was his ability to create pornographic art in a country known for its repression.

"On the Outskirts of Phnom Penh" pg. 34

Under Pol Pot's leadership, it is estimated over two million Cambodians died by execution, forced labor, and famine. Several killing fields were located in the country. We visited the museum and one of the killing fields. The italicized section is in the voice of a guide whose parents were Khmer Rouge.

"World of One Thousand Greens" pg. 53

Animism is the belief that natural objects, natural phenomena, and the universe itself possess souls that may exist apart from their material bodies.

"The Beijing Puppeteer" pg. 58

In the last decade, Beijing has built ten hydroelectric dams and is contemplating more. Thirty million people depend on the Mekong for a living. Its headwaters begin in the plateaus of Tibet. China releases the water when they want to send goods downstream, and shut the dams when they don't need to. This affects the agriculture and fishing industries in Myanmar, Thailand, Laos, Cambodia, and Vietnam.

Hunger to Share is Peg Bresnahan's third collection of poems. She moved to the mountains of Western North Carolina from Wisconsin's Door County Peninsula, exchanging the horizontal waters of Green Bay and Lake Michigan for the land of waterfalls. She received her MFA from Vermont College of Fine Arts in Montpelier. Peg and her husband, sculptor Dan Bresnahan, live next to DuPont State Recreational Forest in Cedar Mountain, sharing the area with deer, snakes, bears, bobcats, fox, opossums, and at least one time a cougar; creatures who've called it home far longer than they have. They have two rescue cats and are hoping to adopt a Doberman to replace their dog Bailey, who died last May—an almost impossible challenge. They enjoy traveling, visiting their families in Wisconsin, Minnesota, California, and one closer to home in North Carolina. This year they plan to explore more of the States, though the appetite to experience other cultures and religions, to travel through countries with names out of history books and fairy tales is difficult to resist.